DISNEP
FROZEN
A Unicorn for Olaf

AUTUMN PUBLISHING

Olaf loved to read. One day, a book with a unicorn on the cover drew his attention. He settled in with one of his best friends, Sven, and read the story aloud.

They both thought it was fantastic. So Olaf read it again. And again. And again.

"Wouldn't it be great to see a unicorn?" asked Olaf.

Sven grunted in agreement.

"Now... where would I live if I were a magical horse with a horn sticking out of my forehead?" asked Olaf. Then, the little snowman gasped.

"The Enchanted Forest, of course! Come on, Sven. Let's go!"

Elsa was petting a baby reindeer when Olaf
and Sven arrived. "What a nice surprise!" she said.
Olaf told Elsa they were on an important quest.
He leant in and whispered, "We're looking for a unicorn."
He asked if she knew where they could find one.
"I don't, but I would love to help you look," said Elsa.

Olaf led the way as the group
set off to find a unicorn.

Soon, they came upon the Earth
Giants, one of the elemental spirits
of the forest. The little snowman
looked up at them and waved.

Then, he had an idea. "Maybe
they can help us get a better view."

Olaf giggled as one of the giants lifted them high into the sky. The forest looked amazing from above, but nobody spotted a unicorn down below.

Olaf pointed at a big white cloud. "That looks like a unicorn."

When the giant set them back down, the Wind Spirit, Gale, whooshed by, tickling Olaf's snow.

"I think someone else wants to help," said Olaf. "Do you like unicorns, Gale?"

Gale whipped around Olaf's twig hairs, swirling them together like a unicorn horn.

The Wind Spirit took off, leading them through the forest. They had to work hard to keep up with Gale!

They stopped in a big open meadow, bursting with colourful flowers.

"This looks like a good spot for a unicorn. They love snails and butterflies," said Olaf. "I read that in a book."

Suddenly, there was a rustling noise and
something moved inside a flower patch!
"Please be a unicorn, please be a unicorn,"
Olaf chanted as he crept over to take a look.

Olaf peered among the flowers and was surprised to see... Bruni, the Fire Spirit!

Bruni joined them and pointed out some hoof prints in the mud. "Those could be unicorn tracks," said Olaf.

They followed the tracks back into the forest, through some shrubs and around a giant oak tree.

When they finally reached the last set of hoof prints they saw... Sven! The reindeer had wandered off in search of a snack.

But that gave Olaf an idea. "Maybe if we were with a unicorn, another one would come out to say hello," he reasoned. Then, he turned to Elsa and whispered his plan.

Elsa smiled and waved her arms, sending her sparkling magic towards Sven.

Olaf admired Elsa's work. "Plan Sven-icorn is going to work," he said, giving the reindeer a pat. "I can feel it."

The group continued through the forest.

As they passed the creek, Olaf saw something reflected in the water's surface... a majestic horse with a long horn!

He quickly turned round to see... the Water Nokk!
His reflection had looked like a unicorn because of a tree
branch behind him.

The Water Spirit wanted to join the group in their search, but it
had been a long day and Olaf was tired. "I don't know," he said.
"Maybe we should go home."

"Come on," said Elsa. "We still have time before it gets dark."

Olaf agreed, and the group continued
to search, heading towards the Dark Sea.

Standing at the shoreline, Olaf turned to his friends. "Thanks for coming with me, everyone," he said. "I'm sorry we didn't find a unicorn—"

"Olaf!" interrupted Elsa.

"It's okay, Elsa," said Olaf. "I'm not sad, because—"

"Olaf!" Elsa said, pointing.

"Elsa," said Olaf. "I'm trying to share my feelings here, and you keep—"

Finally, she took the little snowman's shoulders and turned him round so he could look out to sea.

Olaf gasped as he saw what the rest of them had been staring at: a long, spiralling horn!

The creature leapt above the surface of the water. "It's not a unicorn," said Olaf. "It's a narwhal."

Elsa sighed. "Oh, Olaf—"

Olaf turned to the group, wearing a bright smile. "The narwhal is the unicorn of the sea!" he said, sharing a fun fact. "We found one!"

The group watched the narwhal swim off into the distance before they headed back into the forest.

    As soon as they got back to the castle, Olaf and Sven found Anna and Kristoff.

    "I was wondering where you guys were," said Anna. "Are we going to have story time?"

    "Yes, and I'll tell tonight's story. It's a true adventure," said Olaf. "And it begins with me and Sven."

    Sven was nearly snoring as Kristoff and Anna settled in to listen to the little snowman's tale.